Valyra and the Dragons

Valyra and the Dragons

AND OTHER FANCIFUL ADVENTURE STORIES
Compiled by the Editors
of
Highlights for Children

Compilation copyright © 1994 by Highlights for Children, Inc.
Contents copyright by Highlights for Children, Inc.
Published by Highlights for Children, Inc.
P.O. Box 18201
Columbus, Ohio 43218-0201
Printed in the United States of America.

ISBN 0-87534-619-7

Highlights is a registered trademark of Highlights for Children, Inc.

CONTENTS

CONTENTS

Valyra and the Dragons

By Christiane Kump-Tibbitts

Giggling, Valyra's two older sisters pushed past her into the great hall. It was a livelier gathering of the court than usual, for this was the Eve of Wishes Come True. Valyra remembered the last Eve, when she had been five. Her father had told her that as a young man he had saved the life of Zimbastur, the wizard. In return, the king was allowed a wish, and he chose it with care. Zimbastur granted the wish— that once every seven years the king and all in his family would be given anything they desired.

7

Valyra knew what her sisters would ask for, but they could never have guessed her wish. Valyra had surprised everyone last Eve when she had asked for a golden colt that could gallop on the heels of the wind.

In his flowing blue robe Zimbastur swept into the hall. Valyra's father called for silence. Then Zimbastur began to speak.

"Seven years' turning have once more brought us to the Eve of Wishes Come True. Your Highness, your request is my command."

Valyra listened breathlessly as her father, mother, and sisters each spoke in turn. More land, more jewels, and kings for husbands were their requests. Then all eyes were on her.

She stood tall and looked directly at the wizard. "An adventure is what I want. To journey alone into the Blackcrags and bring back the dragons to live in Heathstone Valley."

There was a gasp throughout the hall.

"It is too dangerous," thundered her father. "I absolutely forbid it."

"Your request has already been granted, Your Highness. Valyra shall have hers also." And from inside his wide sleeve, the wizard drew out a silver conch shell. "Any dragon that hears the sound of this shell will obey your commands. Carry it as you ride your special golden stallion, and I promise no harm will come to you."

Valyra rode forth the next day on her horse, Galderon. By noon, they entered the foothills of the Blackcrag Mountains.

As she crested one of the hills, Valyra spied an armored knight entangled in a huge briar. His horse grazed nearby.

Valyra approached and was unable to restrain a smile. "Do you need help, Sir Knight?"

The knight, who was in a bad humor because of his plight, replied. "Help from a child like you? Ha!"

But Valyra could not leave him this way. She dismounted, and with her sharp dagger she cut the thorny boughs. The knight removed his helmet, staring at her in disbelief. "A girl! I've been rescued from a bramble by a girl!" He shook his head as he went after his horse. Not expecting thanks, Valyra turned once more toward the mountains.

She smiled, thinking about her morning's adventure. When she looked back, the knight still rode at a distance, ignoring her. She felt sure their destinations were the same.

On the high, steep, winding path through the Blackcrags, Galderon was surefooted, but the terrain was hard going for the knight's steed, because of his heavy armor.

As they rounded a bend, Valyra gasped and pulled up the stallion. Before them stretched a narrow gorge, and along one side ran a flat ledge of rock onto which opened several large caves. On the shelf, five silvery green dragons sunned themselves. Overhead, a pair of dragons soared gracefully on great batlike wings.

"I hope you will not be foolish enough to attack them," said the knight, standing behind her.

Valyra whirled around in the saddle. "Attack them? I, Princess Valyra, will bring them back to live in my Heathstone Valley."

The knight smiled mockingly. "Listen, child. Those are fierce, deadly beasts. They tear people to pieces with their claws. And without my help, they will do the same to you. Eldrinore, at your service."

Valyra flushed with anger. "They attack only those who harm them—knights who foolishly try to prove their valor. Dragons are a dying breed, and I intend to protect them."

"What nonsense!"

By this time the dragons were aware of them. Being shy creatures, they retreated into the caves. One large dragon stood guard on the ledge. Eldrinore dismounted, drew his sword, and approached. The dragon flicked its fiery tongue in warning, but the determined knight did not pause.

Flapping its great wings, the dragon spewed out a blast of fire. Eldrinore leaped sideways and forward, swinging his sword. The second fireblast struck him on the shoulder. Even as he fell from the ledge, Valyra put the silver conch shell to her lips and blew. At the sound, the dragon quieted, awaiting her command. Eldrinore's body lay crumpled in pain on a small ledge below.

"Bring him to me," Valyra commanded. "And do not hurt him."

The great creature hovered above Eldrinore and gently lifted him with its claws. When it had laid the knight down before her, Valyra gently told it to return to its home.

"The magic of the shell is great," Eldrinore murmured as he began to regain strength.

"Yet it is useless against one willful, implusive knight's stubbornness," Valyra retorted.

"Not so useless as you think, Your Ladyship. You command the dragons' respect—and mine as well."

Valyra looked toward the caves thoughtfully. "The dragons would probably miss these mountains. Heathstone is not the right place for them to live. What I must do is protect them here."

"I could help you do that," replied Eldrinore, "by blocking this part of the trail with rock. No one will ever see the gorge or the dragon caves again."

"I guess that means me, too."

Eldrinore laughed. "Oh, Valyra, I think nothing could keep you from seeing the dragons again if you set your mind to it."

And Valyra knew he was right.

The Voice from
SHADOO

By Victor Caccamise

Jeff slumped disgustedly at the end of the Tigers' bench. "No hits in five games," he muttered. He kicked at his shadow on the grass.

"Ouch!"

Jeff stared. He kicked again. "Hey! Cut that out!" squeaked the voice.

Jeff got up and walked away from his teammates on the bench. When he was out of hearing range, he said, "Hey! Shadows don't talk!" Suddenly, Jeff saw a scowling face appear on his shadow.

"Let's get something straight," squeaked the voice. "My name is Shadus and I'm your image from the planet Shadoo."

"Aw, come on!" Jeff scoffed. "There's no such planet as Shadoo!"

"Oh no?" Shadus said wisely. "Where do you think your shadow comes from? Shadows come from Shadoo!"

Jeff rubbed his eyes and looked again. The scowling face was still there. "OK, Shadus, so what are you doing here, anyway?"

Shadus scowled even more. "I came down from Shadoo to see if I can't snap you out of the worst case of slump jitters I ever saw!"

"OK," Jeff said. "But how do you know I have slump jitters?"

"Oh, it's no big deal, Jeff. Your miseries are my miseries. You see, I play for the Shaggers in the Shadow Little League on Shadoo. I was doing great until you went into this slump. Now I have the same slump jitters, and I don't like it one bit!"

"I just ran into a little streak of bad luck, that's all, Shadus."

"Bad luck at first, maybe," said Shadus, "but now it's just plain slump jitters!"

Jeff glared at Shadus for a long moment. "OK, Shadus," he said slowly. "I'll try."

"You'd better!" Shadus said, nodding furiously. "Now step up to the platter. I see your leader calling."

Jeff grinned. "You mean step up to the *plate*. The *coach* is calling me."

"Whatever," said Shadus. "I see your group has an occupant on first station."

"Yeah!" Jeff laughed. "A runner on first."

"What is your strategy in this situation?" Shadus asked impatiently.

"I'll bunt the ball down the third-base line so the runner on first can advance to second base," Jeff said. "It might be a sacrifice."

"Risk a sacrifice? Never!" Shadus roared. "No wonder you are in this terrible slump! Bash one over the left barrier and make two scores!"

Jeff bunted and beat the throw to first by a step. He saw the smile on Coach Blake's face. Maybe I'll come out of this slump now, he thought.

Shadus was furious. "That's the worst bash I ever saw! And why are you standing here instead of going on to second station?"

Jeff tried to keep a straight face. "The pitcher would nail me if I did that, Shadus."

"No," shrieked Shadus. "Use a little trickery. Tell the flinger his shoelace is untied. When he leans over to tie it, you advance a station!"

"Is that how you would do it in the shadow league?" Jeff laughed.

"Absolutely," Shadus puffed. "How else can you become king of the group?"

"Haven't you ever heard of teamwork, Shadus?"

"Teamwork?"

"It means playing together as a team, one player helping another. It's called playing winning baseball."

"It's called hunkum bunkum if you ask me!" Shadus scowled. "Now do as I say and advance to second station!"

Jeff prayed for the batter to sock one. And he did, a liner way out to left center.

"Advance! Advance!" shouted Shadus.

Jeff rounded second and started for third. But the ball plunked into the third baseman's glove—right on target—and Jeff was tagged out.

Shadus screamed with disgust. "What is this skidding along on the seat of your pants? What kind of station running do you call this?"

"I had to slide, Shadus," Jeff panted. "it was my only chance to make it."

"If you had stayed on your feet," Shadus roared, "you could have bashed the ball out of the third station's hands and made two scores instead of one!"

"I thought I had a better chance of doing that by sliding," Jeff said with a grin. He was beginning to relax now, thanks to Shadus. "Anyhow," he continued, "we're ahead one to nothing."

The Giants came right back, however, and evened the score in the top of the seventh inning.

The lead-off batter for the Tigers socked the first pitch against the left-field fence for a double. Then it was Jeff's turn to bat. A clean hit would win the game for sure. Jeff stepped into the batter's box, still chuckling at Shadus. He let the first pitch go by for a called strike.

"What in the universe are you waiting for?" Shadus shouted furiously. "You could have bashed that pitch over the barrier!"

Jeff grinned. "The coach signaled for me to take the pitch, to feel out the pitcher."

"The coach?" Shadus groaned. "What does he know? He's not the basher!"

Jeff followed the next pitch perfectly. He swung easily, meeting the ball and lining it safely into left center. The runner on second scored standing up and that was it. The game was over, Tigers two, Giants one. Jeff's teammates mobbed him and carried him off the field. They tousled his hair and slapped him on the back.

"What's all this back-slapping and cheering for such a little bash as that?" Shadus asked.

"It's called team spirit, Shadus," Jeff said.

"Well, your group won the contest, and it seems that you have lost your slump jitters. Perhaps there is something to it at that. I'll suggest that type of baseball to the Shadow League. It's really not much fun trying to be the king of the group anyhow."

Jeff smiled. "No, being a team player is better."

"Well," Shadus said, "I guess my work is done here. You can kick your shadow all you want to now, Jeff."

Just to make sure, Jeff waited a moment and kicked at his shadow. At that instant he heard a swishing sound, and when he looked up, he saw a small black cloud shaped like a baseball disappearing into the clear blue sky.

DINOSAUR RANCH

By Douglas Borton

Toby didn't catch sight of the tyrannosaur until he'd ridden around a bend in the canyon trail. By then it was too late.

He reined up hard on Bigfoot, the birdlike dinosaur that served as his mount, and stared at the huge meat-eater. The Tyrant Lizard's toothy skull bobbed eighteen feet above the ground. Its two tiny fore-claws twitched, and its long, gray-green tail swished, brushing away a buzzing cloud of gnats like a gust of hot air.

Bigfoot bucked and hissed. Toby patted the ornithomimid's tough, leathery hide to keep the animal from bolting in panic.

"Easy, boy. Easy," Toby whispered. He knew there was no point in trying to run. Like all ostrich dinosaurs, Bigfoot could put on a burst of speed but would tire quickly. *Tyrannosaurus rex* had less speed but great stamina, and was relentless in pursuit of its prey.

The tyrannosaur took a step toward him, sniffing noisily, its tongue gliding along the row of seven-inch fangs crowding its mouth. Toby's heart thumped and sweat ran from his forehead.

All this was his fault, of course. He shouldn't have taken the shortcut through the canyon on his way back to Dinosaur Ranch. He'd gotten careless, and carelessness, as his mom often reminded him, was the one mistake you could not afford to make. Not here. Not in this world.

It was a harsh world never meant for human beings. There would be no people here at all if not for the invention of time travel in the first decade of the twenty-second century. Crossing a time-bridge between the future and the past, a band of scientists had set up a colony in the Cretaceous Period, millions of years before the dawn of history.

Then something had gone terribly wrong. For reasons unknown, the time-bridge winked out, stranding the colonists and cutting them off from civilization. Their supplies of food and power cells quickly ran out. They'd had no choice but to build a new life for themselves, living off the land as pioneers had done in other lands and other times.

All of that had taken place twenty years ago, before Toby was even born. Just last month he had turned eleven. This was the only home he'd ever known, this primeval forest scored by canyons and stretching to purple mountain ranges that loomed like frozen storm clouds on every horizon.

To Toby, it was only natural that ranchers should herd and brand dinosaurs, roping and riding the smaller plant-eaters and raising the bigger ones as cattle. He found nothing unusual about the ranch's sturdy cattle pens, crowded with bleating duckbills and braying ankylosaurs.

He'd grown accustomed to watching ranch hands return with an iguanodon, a corythosaur, or even a horned triceratops lashed in their lassoes. Someday Toby would join them. When he did, he'd use the lasso on his belt for more than the rope tricks he practiced now.

He'd join them, all right—but only if he could get out of the mess he was in. He had to think. In times of trouble, his dad always said, think clearly. Animals have instincts to help them out of a jam. People were different. They had to use their wits.

Toby was still thinking when, with a surprising burst of speed, the Tyrannosaurus charged.

Bigfoot wheeled, squawking in terror, and broke into a sprint. The ostrich dinosaur's legs were a blur. His long, skinny tail jerked from side to side to help him maintain his balance.

Bouncing in the saddle, Toby looked over his shoulder and saw the tyrannosaur in pursuit.

Already Bigfoot was slowing down as his energy ebbed. Toby glanced back again. The striding tyrannosaur was closing the gap between them.

Think, he told himself. Come on, Toby, think! Then, up ahead, he saw his chance.

On one side of the trail a huge boulder sat precariously balanced on an eroded pedestal of rock. Toby tossed his lasso and caught the boulder with a lucky, perfect throw. He pulled Bigfoot to a halt and knotted the other end of the rope around a towering cycad on the opposite side of the trail. The rope was stretched between the boulder and the tree.

This had better work. It *had* to work, Toby thought fearfully.

Sensing easy prey, the Tyrannosaurus barreled forward. Its jaws snapped hungrily, spraying flecks of foam. The canyon shook with the giant's echoing footsteps.

The meat-eater was thirty feet from Toby when it hit the rope, jerking the line taut. The boulder tumbled off its pedestal, crashing down in a cloud of dust. For a second, Toby couldn't tell what had happened to the Tyrannosaurus.

The dust cleared to reveal the tyrannosaur stumbling in circles, howling in frustration and rage. The boulder had landed on its tail, pinning it to the ground. The Tyrant Lizard wouldn't chase them anymore today.

Toby let out a shaky sigh of relief and patted Bigfoot on the head. The ornithomimid shook his head and grunted contentedly.

"Come on, boy. Let's go home. Supper's waiting."

Riding back to the ranch, Toby remembered stories he'd heard about the world his parents had been raised in. It was hard to imagine a world that had no dinosaurs.

Maybe someday, Toby thought, a scientist would discover the bones of a Tyrannosaurus with a broken tail. And in that far-off world, the scientist would scratch his head and wonder.

The
Fourth
Wish

By Randall Heeres

Charlotte didn't know what to do with her fourth wish.

She had read stories about children granted three wishes by a magical fairy or by an old genie who lived in a dusty lamp. Charlotte had often thought about what her three wishes would be, just in case. So by the time Charlotte found the magical marble in the barn, she was ready.

At first, she hadn't known that the marble was magical, but when she polished its gold surface—

Poof!—right there in Uncle Al's barn stood a genuine gigantic genie.

"I AM MAGRIDD!" the genie bellowed loudly enough to startle the cows and shake pieces of straw loose from the loft above. "What is it that you desire?" Charlotte's surprise must have shown on her freckled face.

"Haven't you ever seen a genie before, young lady?" asked Magridd. His red beard curled almost to the barn floor. He had big black eyes, and a green turban was wound around his head.

"You have three wishes, like the others," said the genie, his eyes flashing. "But today is my birthday. I am four thousand years old. So, in honor of me, you are awarded a fourth wish."

Charlotte was ready for three wishes, but what in the world would she do with a fourth one? I'll make three wishes first, she thought, and see if this genie is for real.

"I would like a blue bicycle," Charlotte told Magridd, "with a loud horn and three lights."

Poof!

Before Charlotte could say "please," a shiny blue bike was standing next to her on the barn floor. Charlotte climbed aboard her new bicycle. The horn blast made dust fall from the rafters. She was truly, truly delighted.

"Now I want a new tractor for my Uncle Al. His is so . . ."

Poof! Poof!

Before Charlotte could say "old and broken-down," there was a red tractor outside—the very one Uncle Al had wanted at the dealership.

"Uncle Al will just love this!" Charlotte exclaimed.

Magridd nodded in approval, twirling his red beard between his long, bony fingers.

"Now, young lady, make your third wish. I must hurry along. I have a birthday party to attend." Magridd looked down his thick nose at Charlotte.

"A dog," she said.

"Any special kind?" asked Magridd.

"Oh, a beagle. Or a cocker spaniel. Or . . ."

"Young lady, you *must* make up your mind. I don't have all century." Magridd sighed impatiently and checked the small hourglass strapped to his blue sash.

"A collie!" Charlotte blurted.

Poof! Poof! Poof!

Before Charlotte could say "brown and white," the collie was rubbing against her overalls. Charlotte bent to pet her new pup.

"I'll call you Magic," she said, burying her face in the puppy's brown and white fur. Magic licked her hand and wagged his tail with glee.

"And your fourth wish?" Magridd folded his arms. "I must leave soon."

"I can't think of a fourth wish," Charlotte said. "I thought you always gave just three."

"I already explained that," Magridd said, scowling at his hourglass and then at Charlotte.

"Could I just ask my uncle?" Charlotte pleaded.

"NO!"

The genie's voice shook the barn. Magic crawled behind Charlotte's legs and whimpered.

"Well, then, I . . . ," Charlotte began. Then an idea flashed into her head. Her eyes started to twinkle.

"I wish," Charlotte said, "for you to come back here in one year and grant me four more wishes."

Charlotte watched the giant genie closely.

Magridd glared at her. He shifted from one foot to the other. He stroked his red beard. He looked up at the roof and then down at the floor.

Finally, Magridd boomed a laugh. "I admire a good idea when I hear one," he said. "And I bet I can already guess what your fourth wish will be next year."

Charlotte smiled.

The genie *poofed* back inside the gold marble.

Charlotte pushed the shiny marble deep into the pocket of her overalls. She whistled to her pup and rode her new bike toward the cornfield to tell Uncle Al about the tractor.

And to plan her three wishes for next year.

CODE RED

By Paul E. Stawski

The first thought that struck Becky when she awoke was how quiet everything seemed on board the spacecraft. She didn't hear any of the others. The only sound was the constant low hum of the ship as it found its way among the stars.

Startled, she jumped and called, "Anybody here?"

Quickly, Becky connected the ship's voice controls and asked about the rest of the crew. The ship's computer-voice, Comptrol, answered in perfect, understandable English.

"They're in space sleep," it said.

"All of them?" she asked. "Then why did you wake me?"

"Code Red," Comptrol replied.

Becky's eyes widened. She knew what Code Red meant and the extreme danger they were in. Alien ships were nearby.

"When will they get here?" she asked, her voice trembling slightly.

"One hour," said Comptrol, "and counting."

Becky tried to sound unafraid. "Then you've got to wake the others," she said.

There was no answer.

"I'm only nine years old!" she screamed.

"Age," said Comptrol, "has nothing to do with it. Under Code Red conditions, I am required to awaken one crew member. I chose you."

"But I've never been in a Code Red before!" Becky cried.

"You've done very well in practice," said Comptrol.

Becky put her head down and started to cry. Yes, she thought, I did do well in practice. But that was only a video game! This is real life. And this time their lives depended on it. Besides, Jim had been better in practice than she was, and he was a grown-up. He'd know what to do. Why didn't the ship's computer wake him?

"Code Red, Code Red," said Comptrol again, interrupting her thoughts.

Becky lifted her head and looked around the ship through blurry, tear-filled eyes. *Code Red,* she thought to herself, as she saw the rest of the crew unmoving in their space sleep. And it's all up to me.

Becky sat at the video game—practicing, pressing buttons, working hard at destroying the game's enemy spaceships. She had won three out of the last five games. But that meant she had lost twice—two times the ship and Becky's crew mates wouldn't have made it in real life.

"How much time left?" she asked.

"Nineteen minutes," said Comptrol.

She cleared the screen and started the game again. This was silly! Even if she won every game, how could she be sure she'd win when it really counted—in real life?

Nobody won every time. Not even Jim. Sure, you could decide to let the computer run the game, but then all you could do was watch. None of the crew ever let the computer do that, except . . . except her, she thought.

Becky's mind whirled. Things just didn't make sense. When she let the computer play, it often did just as poorly as anyone else. So how could letting it take over now help?

"Code Red," said Comptrol. "Three minutes and counting down."

Becky ran her fingers through her hair in one quick, nervous motion. Then hesitantly she took over the controls and flipped the switch from GAME to ON/EMERGENCY.

"Code Red," said Comptrol again. "Two minutes and counting."

Rapidly Becky pressed buttons that gave commands. PREPARE DEFENSE WEAPONS. ALL SYSTEMS ALERT. Her fingers danced over the controls until she came upon the button that said FIRE.

She hesitated and thought for a moment about the alien ships. Who was in them? Were they beings who wanted to destroy her ship, or would they let her pass if she didn't fire at them first? What if—just what if—the aliens were as frightened as she was? Did she have a right to destroy them for that?

"Code Red," said Comptrol. "One minute and counting 60, 59, 58 . . ."

Becky searched the computer panel for the HOLD FIRE button. "I'm sorry," she said to the sleeping crew as she pressed the button. "I hope I'm not letting you down." Now, she knew, it was out of her hands.

She watched the screen as it filled with the glowing dots of alien ships. What now? she wondered.

"Code Red," said Comptrol. "Zero."

She waited anxiously as the dot that indicated her own spaceship moved slowly ahead. And as her ship passed the last alien ship, Becky broke into a long sigh of relief. Not one ship had fired. They were safe.

"I did it!" she yelled through her tears. "*We* did it! Thanks, Comptrol, for choosing me!"

"Code Red over," said Comptrol.

Becky smiled and wiped the tears from her eyes.

"You knew what I'd do all along, didn't you?" she asked with a sigh.

Comptrol didn't answer. It didn't have to. Becky knew the truth. As she climbed into bed and slipped into space sleep, there was nothing more she needed to know.

The Seventh
POTATO

By Ivy O. Eastwick

Joe's mother was upset.

"Just look!" she said to no one in particular. "Just look at these potatoes. They are so expensive, and yet the grocer has put half a dozen *seed* potatoes into my bag. Seed potatoes! What was he thinking—whoever can cook seed potatoes?"

Joe looked inside his mother's shopping bag. Mixed in with the good potatoes, he saw seven little ones with tiny sprouts coming through their brown skins. Joe thought they looked interesting.

"Take them outside, Joe, and throw them into the trash can. I can't cook these."

Joe took the seven small, sprouting potatoes from his mother and carried them into the yard.

Before putting them into the trash, he looked at them closely. One looked as if it had a face, a little, brown, smiling face and two laughing eyes.

It also looked as if it had two arms, for two of its little sprouts were outstretched.

"I'm not throwing *you* away," said Joe to the Seventh Potato. "I'm going to plant you in this corner. By the wall."

And that is what he did.

Well, most potatoes are just potatoes. But a potato with a brown head, a smiling face, two eyes, and two outstretched arms is a very different thing.

With such a potato as the Seventh Potato, anything may happen. And it did.

No sooner was it underground than the Seventh Potato's sprouts began to grow. And though there was no one to see, the grin on the Seventh Potato's face grew wider . . . and wider . . . and wider!

That night while Joe and his parents slept, the Seventh Potato pushed up . . . and up . . . and up!

The next morning Joe heard his mother call, "Joe! Joe! Come here quickly."

Joe and Big Joe, his father, hurried downstairs.

What *could* have happened to make Joe's mother sound so excited?

"Look!" she said, pointing out the window.

They both followed her finger's direction.

"It's a tree," said Big Joe slowly.

"I know it's a tree! But *what* tree? We didn't have a tree in the garden last night."

Joe suddenly realized what had happened. The tree was growing in exactly the same place where he had planted the Seventh Potato.

So he explained, "It's a potato tree."

"There's no such thing as a potato tree," said his mother with exasperation in her voice.

Big Joe had grown up in the country, and now he said slowly, "I must say it *does* look like a potato plant. A *giant* potato plant. Look at its purple and white flowers. They're just like the flowers that grow on potato plants."

Joe's mother shook her head. "Whoever heard of a potato tree?" she said. "I don't like it. Big Joe, take the ax and chop it down."

"Oh, no!" protested Little Joe. "It's my own good little potato tree that I planted myself."

"Don't talk nonsense," said his mother. "Big Joe . . ."

But Joe's father liked the look of the potato tree and, besides, he knew that Joe wanted the tree.

When Joe's mother saw that they were going to be obstinate, she sighed and said, "Oh, all right! Potato tree indeed!"

Under the dark ground, the Seventh Potato heard. Nobody saw, of course, but he grinned a wide grin.

He even giggled a bit, though nobody heard except the worms living underground.

He intended to surprise the family even more.

One day the flowers on the potato tree began to wither and fall. The wind blew them far away.

Joe's mother watched them go.

"Now what?" she asked her family.

Big Joe thought for a moment and then said, "Large potatoes . . . perhaps . . ."

Little Joe said nothing. He just watched and waited. Each morning he was the first to rise, the first to fly downstairs, the first to dash into the garden.

For three weeks nothing happened to the potato tree. And then, one morning . . .

Joe was the first downstairs as usual. "Mother! Father! Quick. Come quickly."

Joe's parents tumbled out of bed and hurried downstairs. Joe was in the garden. They joined him there. Like Joe, they stood there staring . . . and staring . . . and staring!

The branches of the potato tree bowed nearly to the ground with melons, apples, plums, peaches, apricots, grapes, pears, and nectarines.

"Oh," sighed Joe, "I knew the Seventh Potato was a magic potato, but I never thought that it would do anything like this."

And deep, deep down under the ground the Seventh Potato laughed . . . and laughed . . . and laughed!

Though, of course, only the worms heard.

The Red Flower

By Janet S. Anderson

Once there was a princess named Tara. Every day Tara walked sadly in the garden. Every day she knelt by the stream to pick a rose for her mother.

Her mother, the queen, was very sick. The royal doctor gave the queen medicine. The royal wizard chanted spells. Nothing helped.

One day Tara saw a spider's web. Caught in it was a tiny caterpillar, struggling to free itself. Gently, Tara pulled it from the web and set it in the grass. Suddenly, a beautiful butterfly hovered near her ear.

"You are most kind," said the butterfly. "Now I will help *you*. At the top of the mountain, you will find something to make your mother well again."

Tara's heart leaped with joy. But she looked at the mountain. It looked very high. "How will I get there?" she asked.

"Take this path," said the butterfly. "You must walk on and on, until you reach the river."

Tara started down the path. It became rough and full of brambles. Once she fell. Her dress became torn and dirty. But she walked on and on until she reached the river.

"Butterfly?" she called, but it was gone. The river was wide and deep. "How will I ever get across?" said Tara.

"You must swim," said a new, deeper voice. It was another butterfly, larger and more beautiful than the first. "You must swim on and on, until you reach the far shore."

Tara waded into the water. It was very cold. "I can't . . . ," she said. Then she looked up. The high mountain gleamed. Up there was something to make her mother well.

She began to swim. The water was cold, and the current was strong. But she swam on and on until she reached the far shore.

"Butterfly?" she called, but it was gone. Around her loomed the foothills, dark and steep. "Where do I go?" said Tara.

"Come," said a new voice beside her. It was a third butterfly, larger and even more beautiful than the second. "Here is the trail. You must climb up and up until you can go no farther."

Tara started up the trail. It was steep and rocky. Tara was tired. Her feet were bruised and sore. But she climbed up and up, until she could go no farther. Between her and the mountain's peak lay a deep chasm.

"Butterfly?" she called, but it was gone. "There is no way across," said Tara. "There is no way to reach the mountain's peak."

"There is a way," said a voice. It was yet another butterfly, an enormous butterfly with huge, gleaming wings. "You must fly," said the butterfly. "You must fly with me, up and up to the highest peak."

Tara climbed onto the butterfly's back. She clung tightly. Below her swirled rocks and waterfalls. The butterfly flew up and up. At the top of the peak a red flower held its face to the last rays of the sun.

"Pick it," said the butterfly, hovering. "Each year a new bloom takes its place." Tara reached down and picked the flower. It glowed like a ruby in her trembling hand.

"Now you must hurry," said the butterfly. "Your mother must hold it before the full moon rises." Down they plunged into the twilight. Down, down they flew to the bank of the river. "Swim," the butterfly said and was gone.

Holding the flower tightly, Tara waded into the deep river. She began to swim, but suddenly the current gave a strong pull. It pulled the flower from her hand. Away the flower swirled, over a waterfall and down the dark river.

Weeping, Tara climbed from the cold water and stumbled down the path. The day grew darker. The sun set. Finally, Tara could go no farther. Still weeping, she crept close to a tree and fell asleep. Slowly the full moon rose and bathed the darkening forest in its gentle light.

Tara woke up. The path gleamed like a ribbon through the trees. Sadly, she followed it home. She had failed. Tara stepped across the stream and into the garden.

Her mother sat beside the rosebush, smiling, and in her hand was a red flower. It was not a rose. Her mother held out her arms, and Tara ran to her.

"That red flower," said Tara. "Where on earth did you find it?"

"I was told that you were missing from the garden," said her mother. "They brought me here, to lie beside the stream and await your return. As I lay here, ill and worried, the day began to grow dark. And just as the sun set, this flower came drifting by.

"It drifted close to my hand and looked so beautiful that I plucked it out. The blossom smelled of the mountains and of the river and of the forest. It was as though I held all of nature in my hand. And as I held it, my weakness left me. I began to feel strong again. I am well, and you are home." Gently she stroked Tara's snarled hair. "I won't ask you where you've been. I feel as if I know."

Together they looked at the mountain, angled high against the moon. Wings brushed softly above their heads. "An owl, perhaps," said the queen. "Come, it is time to go inside."

As Tara followed her mother, the princess raised her hand to the night sky. Wings fluttered in return and were gone.

THE DAY THE BOOKS LEAKED

By Gene Twaronite

Elwyn knew something was wrong when he started to read from his favorite book, *Alice in Wonderland:* "Alice was beginning to get . . ."

"To get what?" said Elwyn. He stared at a big white space on the first page. It was as if someone had ripped the rest of the words right off the page.

Elwyn flipped through the book. There were white spaces on every page. Almost half of the words were gone and, worst of all, it was a book he had borrowed from the library.

As Elwyn watched, the word *caterpillar* began to wriggle on the page, then flew into the air and straight through his bedroom wall. He shut the book, but it was no use. The words *orange marmalade* oozed right after the caterpillar.

Elwyn ran all the way to the library. A cloud of words dribbled out behind him. He opened the book and showed the pages to the librarian, Mr. Gryphon. They were now completely blank.

"Something's happened to the words," said Elwyn in a shaky voice. "They're gone."

Mr. Gryphon peered over his glasses and frowned. "Words don't just get up and go," he said. "What did you do to this book?"

"Nothing," said Elwyn. "The words just leaked out! Maybe you should check the other books."

"That's the silliest thing I've ever heard," said Mr. Gryphon. He opened a book on his desk.

The page was full of white spaces.

As Mr. Gryphon looked up, a string of words fluttered like butterflies past his beaked nose.

"My word!" he said. "I've never seen anything like this in all my years as a librarian."

He and Elwyn ran through the stacks. Words were seeping from every shelf and floating down the aisles. Some of the books were blank, but some were missing only a few words.

"This is terrible," Mr. Gryphon said. "What good is a book with missing words?"

"Don't worry," said Elwyn. "I'll find out what's causing the leak." With that, he followed the word *serendipity* as it snaked out the front door.

Outside, *serendipity* floated away and joined other words that swarmed in all types and sizes through the sky like a squiggling black cloud. They all seemed to be heading downtown.

Elwyn followed the swarm down East Street. He noticed swarms of words coming from different parts of the city.

Suddenly there was a crash, as two cars collided at the corner of East and South Streets. One of the drivers hadn't stopped for the sign because the word *STOP* was gone.

So it's not just books that are leaking, thought Elwyn. Everywhere he looked there were blank street signs, storefronts, and billboards. There were cars honking and people yelling at each other. No one knew when to stop or go, or where to find anything.

Farther down East Street, Elwyn saw an angry man on a park bench flipping through a newspaper that had only pictures and pieces of stories.

Why should only *some* of the words be leaking? wondered Elwyn. He turned onto Main Street and was almost trampled by a crowd of angry people. "Give us back our words!" the people shouted.

Overhead, the words had come together in one big swarm that looked like the funnel-shaped cloud of a giant tornado. The swarm was being pulled down through the roof of the *Beagle Daily News.* Whatever is causing the leak, Elwyn thought, must be very near.

Elwyn pushed his way through the crowd and went inside to the newsroom. He knocked on the editor's door.

"What is it?" asked the editor.

"Something is making all the words in town swarm through the sky and fly into your building," said Elwyn.

"Sure," said the editor. "Now go follow your words someplace else. We have enough words around here. Too many, if you ask me."

Just then a reporter ran into the office, screaming, "What have you done to my story?" He handed the editor a sheet of paper that was blank except for adverbs and adjectives like *very* and *great.*

"I don't understand," said the editor. "We had the computer programmed to delete unnecessary words from our stories. It doesn't seem to be working."

"Where is this computer?" asked Elwyn.

"The mainframe is in the next room," said the editor. "It's one of the most powerful computers money can buy."

They entered the room and stared at the computer's big display screen. Lines of words were zipping across its face and disappearing, faster than rabbits down a hole.

"Can the computer display the new program?" asked Elwyn.

"Sure," said the editor. She entered a command. "DELETE ALL NECESSARY WORDS" appeared on the screen.

"There's your problem," said Elwyn. "The computer has been given the wrong instructions. It's erasing all the *necessary* words. And it's pulling them here from all over town!"

"I'll call the programmer," said the editor.

"There's no time for that," said Elwyn. "Do you mind if I try something?"

"Anything!" said the editor.

Elwyn entered a new command into the computer: "INSERT ALL NECESSARY WORDS."

Suddenly words began marching backward on the screen. From its memory, the computer replaced all the necessary words it had erased. As if by magic, they swirled out the roof and went squiggling back into place, all over town.

Outside, people again knew when to stop and go, and where to find things. Best of all, they could read their favorite books again.

Elwyn returned to the library to find Mr. Gryphon watching words flow back where they belonged.

"Isn't it wonderful?" he said. "How did you do it?"

"It's simple, Mr. Gryphon," said Elwyn. "You just need to know the necessary words."

CROSSING THE FRONTIER

by Beth Thompson

"Grandma, look at these neat space bunks. That's where we'll sleep in Home Base One," Jeremy said excitedly, pointing to the hammocks in a photograph of the space station.

"And here's a picture of the lab where Mom and Dad work. It's in the second module," added his sister Tanya. "The three modules are like gigantic metal sausages linked together in a circle," she explained. "One is for living, one is for lab work and experiments, and one is for equipment."

Grandma Frazier sighed. "Well, it all looks fascinating, but I wish you two wouldn't be gone for so long. And so far away, too—in outer space!"

"Dad says we're pioneers in space, just like the old-time pioneers who crossed the prairies going out West," said Jeremy. "Only we'll travel in the space station instead of a covered wagon."

"And instead of cooking our meals over a campfire," said Tanya, "we'll be eating freeze-dried food from little packages. All we have to add is hot water to get beef stew or green beans . . ."

"Or pumpkin pie!" Jeremy grinned. "Wish you could send some of your great brownies dried in a package, Grandma. We'll miss them."

"And we'll really miss you, Grandma," said Tanya.

The children's parents were both scientists who spent months at a time working in the lab of Home Base One, which was orbiting the earth. Usually Jeremy and Tanya stayed with their grandmother, watching news about the station on television. This time, however, the children were going, too, and the Fraziers would be one of the first families to live together in a space station.

"I'll miss you both," said Grandma Frazier, "but I know you'll have lots to tell me when you get back. And here's something to take with you on the trip." She handed them a small package wrapped in brown paper. "Don't open it until you get there!" she added.

On the way home from Grandma's house the children wondered what could be in the small package. Jeremy sniffed it. "Well, it's not brownies!"

"Maybe it's a video cassette for the viewing screen," said Tanya eagerly. The children would be using the computer in the living module to do their homework, and for fun they would watch movies on the video screen or listen to audio-taped books and stories on the headphones.

In the excitement of getting ready to go, the children forgot about the little package. It was tucked away in Tanya's duffel bag when she boarded the spacecraft, buckled herself in place, and waited for the roar of the rockets to signal lift-off.

After they arrived at Home Base One, Tanya and Jeremy eagerly explored their new home.

"Watch me!" shouted Tanya, floating weightlessly across the room. Jeremy quickly joined her. By the end of the first day they were tired, so they sat down to watch a movie on the video monitor.

Suddenly, the picture on the screen faded, and the lights in the module dimmed.

"Looks like trouble with the solar cells," said Dad. "We won't have anything but the emergency lights if we can't repair them. You two stay here, and leave everything turned off. I'll call on the intercom when we get it fixed." He and Mom followed the other scientists through the narrow passageway into the third module.

It was quiet in the dimly lit module. "Jeremy, I'm scared," said Tanya. "What will happen if they can't repair the cells?"

"Mom and Dad won't let us down," Jeremy insisted. "They never do. Remember that time the lights went off at home during a storm? They had to rig up something with the transporter battery, but they did get lights going for us."

"It may take a long time, though," Tanya said. "I wish we could call Grandma, the way we did last time." Thinking of Grandma Frazier reminded Tanya of the little package. She tugged it out of her duffel bag and ripped off the paper, carefully tucking it away so it wouldn't float around the module.

"Oh, it's just a book," Jeremy said. "Books are so old-fashioned."

"But look, Jeremy. This is a diary written by a pioneer girl in 1855. Why, that's over a hundred and fifty years ago. And there are two little notebooks, too. I wonder what they're for?"

Tanya opened the book and read aloud:

"'September 22, 1855. It's cold tonight, and Pa says we must hurry so we won't get trapped by the snow. Our wagon broke crossing the river, and Pa has been working for three days to repair the wheel. I'm sitting by the campfire while Ma puts Baby Sara to bed. It's lonely out here, so quiet and still, with only the stars overhead and you to write in, little book. You are a comfort.'"

Tanya stopped and stared out the window at the darkness of space. "You know, Jeremy, these are the same stars she watched that night. I feel as if we've just met a new friend."

Jeremy nodded, reaching for one of the notebooks. "I'm going to write about *our* trip," he said, "and maybe in another hundred years a pioneer traveling out through the Milky Way will read about our adventure on the frontier of space."

"January 18, 2015," he wrote. "We are aboard Home Base One, waiting for the solar cells to be repaired and watching the stars . . ."

The Listening Shell

By M. Donnaleen Howitt

Daniel lived on a little island with his grandparents. One day he found a beautiful shell. It was shaped like a cone, and was rough and white on the outside. Inside, it was pink and shiny.

He showed the shell to his grandfather, who said, "This is a listening shell. If you hold it up to your ear, you will hear the sound of the ocean waves."

Daniel tried to hear the sound, but the real waves made too much noise. "I'll put the shell in this quiet cave." he said. "I'll come back later to listen."

Daniel often helped his grandfather fish in the bay and cut wood, and he held up the yarn for his grandmother when she wound it for knitting. He had a little boat and a sturdy tree house that his grandfather had helped him build. There were oysters in the bay and small animals in the woods, but Daniel was lonely.

One day Daniel went back to the cave. It was in the side of a cliff, away from the sounds of the shore. He held the shell to his ear.

"Swoosh-swish!" said the shell as Daniel listened.

"Swoosh-swish. Who is this?"

"It's me—Daniel."

"Swoosh-swish. What do you wish?"

"What do you mean?" said Daniel.

"Swoosh-swish. Tell me your wish," said the shell.

Daniel's eyes grew big. He thought for a long time, then put the shell to his ear.

"Swoosh-swish. What do you wish?"

"I'm lonely," said Daniel. "I would like a dog to keep me company."

"Go home and see," said the shell. "But listen to me. Never tell about the shell."

Daniel ran up the cliffside along the path to the cottage where he lived. His grandmother stood at the door. Beside her was a dog, wagging its tail.

"Look what has come to our cottage," Grandmother said. "How could this little brown dog get to our island?"

Daniel clapped his hands and whistled. The little dog came to his side.

"I'll call you Answer. You're the answer to a wish I made."

For many days Daniel and Answer played together on the shore and in the woods. Daniel was no longer lonely, but he was tired of the island. He went again to the cave.

"Swoosh-swish," said the shell to Daniel. "What do you wish?"

"I would like to see new places and meet new friends, but we are too poor," said Daniel.

"Indeed? Indeed? In the bay lies what you need," said the shell.

Daniel and Answer scooped two oysters from the bay. In each of them they found a pearl.

Daniel returned to the shell.

"Swoosh-swish. What do you wish?"

"There is a land across the water. I want to go there. I would like to make new friends."

"Pack a bag and get your kite. Take me with you on your flight," said the shell.

"Flight?" said Daniel. "My kite won't carry me! I'm too heavy!"

"If you think you will fall, you will not fly at all. Now go away and do as I say."

Daniel packed a little bag and got his kite. He put the shell into his bag, and gave Answer a pat. Then he stood on the cliff and held tight to the kite string.

The kite lifted into the wind, and soon Daniel was flying over the bay. On the far shore he saw a city.

The kite lowered him into the midst of a great fair. The colors and sounds thrilled Daniel. He carried his kite and bag past booths and past tents. He watched some acrobats and animals performing in front of a large tent. When they went inside, Daniel tried to follow.

A tall man with a huge mustache and a top hat stopped him. "You must pay to go inside, my little friend!"

"Friend!" thought Daniel. "How very nice! I have a friend."

He felt in his pocket for a pearl. "Will this be enough?" he asked the man.

"Ah!" said the man as he quickly took the pearl. "This will be fine. Are you alone?"

"Yes," said Daniel. "But I hope to find some friends."

The man twirled his mustache, tipped his hat, and said, "You have found one. Enjoy the show."

Daniel clapped and cheered as he watched dancing bears and tumbling monkeys. When the show was over, he met the man again.

"I'm very hungry," said Daniel.

"Do you have another pearl to pay for food?" the man asked.

Daniel held up his other pearl. "Will this do?" he asked shyly.

"Very nicely," the man said as he plucked the pearl from Daniel's fingers. "Come along."

After the meal Daniel was sleepy. The fair lights were turning off. "I need a place to sleep, my friend," he said.

"You must pay," said the man.

"But I have no more pearls," said Daniel.

"Too bad." The man tipped his hat and left.

Huddled beside the dark tents, Daniel was lonely and cold. He reached into his bag for the warm sweater his grandmother had knit for him. His hand touched the listening shell, and he held it to his ear.

"Swoosh-swish. What do you wish?" said the shell. "Think hard and think fast. This wish will be your last!"

Daniel thought hard about the island. He thought of his grandfather, who had made the kite, and of his grandmother, who had made his sweater. He thought of Answer, who was such a true friend. He began to cry.

"I wish to go back to my little island," he said.

When the kite lowered him on the shore of the island, Daniel placed the shell in its cave and ran home to his cozy bed.

For many months Daniel and Answer played happily together. One day Answer chased a chipmunk into the cave where the shell was. Daniel followed, and held the shell to his ear.

"Swoosh-swish, swoosh-swish," said the shell. And nothing, nothing more.

Uletka and the White Lizard

By Iris Simon

Princess Uletka ran down the steps of the castle and threw her arms around her father.

"Come back soon," she said.

He kissed her cheek. "As soon as I can. While I'm gone, there is something I want you to do. Here is the key to the stone tower at the end of the garden. There is a white lizard in a cage in the tower. Every day give the lizard food and water. But you must promise me never to open the cage or take the lizard out of the tower."

"I promise," said Uletka. Her father gave her one last kiss. Then he mounted his horse and was gone on his journey.

As soon as he left, Uletka ran to see the lizard. It was slim and smooth, with eyes the color of turquoise. It ran around the cage and played with a straw she held out to it.

Suddenly the lizard sat still and stared at her. "What a lovely fairy you are!" it said.

"I'm not a fairy," said Uletka. "I'm a girl."

"How odd," the lizard said. "I was sure you were a fairy. Now if I had my magic cloak, I would throw it over your shoulders, and you would become a fairy right away. You would be able to appear and disappear. You could change yourself into anything you wanted to be. You could go anywhere in the world and see everything."

"I would love that," Uletka said. "Do you really think that I could become a fairy?"

"Of course," said the lizard. "Oh, dear, if only I could get out of this cage! I know just where the cloak is—and my magic wand, too. If you would let me out for a little while, I could get them and be right back here in an instant."

Uletka was so excited at the thought of the magic cloak that she forgot all about her promise. She opened the cage, and out jumped the lizard. As soon as its feet touched the ground, it changed into an evil witch with wild hair and flashing eyes. The witch waved her hand, and Uletka shrank to the size of a mouse. The witch laughed and chased her out of the castle and into the forest.

Uletka ran until she stumbled against a tree. In its trunk was a door. Uletka turned the handle and went in. There, in the heart of the tree, was a room with a chair, a table, and a bed. On the table were dishes of nuts, berries, and honey. Uletka was hungry. She ate, then lay down and fell asleep.

Uletka stayed in the tree. Every day she gathered nuts and berries for dinner. She drank from a nearby spring. Often she would lie in the grass, watching the small animals and insects. She most enjoyed seeing the furry yellow bees climb in and out of the flowers. After a while they seemed to know her and would greet her before going back to their hive.

A blackbird who became her friend carried her on his back when he flew about the woods. He often sang to her. But Uletka missed her father and mother. She longed for her home. The blackbird was sorry for her and wanted to help.

"Uletka," he said, "if you still have the key to the tower, perhaps we can lock up the witch again."

"Yes, I still have the key. At least we can try— maybe luck will be with us."

They made careful plans. Uletka filled a bag with nuts and berries, and made a water flask from an acorn shell. They set off the next morning for the tower, knowing that the witch, who watched Uletka constantly, would follow to find out what they were going to do.

They traveled most of the day. At dinnertime they stopped by a lake covered with water lilies. Uletka was refilling her water flask when she noticed that the air had become very still. The sky grew dark. The hush was broken by the rustling of leaves, as though a wind were blowing.

"The witch is coming," the blackbird screamed. Uletka grabbed her things and ran. The bird flew ahead of her. They could hear the witch's cackling laugh close behind them.

A bee on the way to its hive recognized Uletka. It flew home and danced a message to the other bees. Buzzing loudly, they flew at the witch. They blocked her path and stung her. Surprised by the bees' attack, the witch dropped her wand, and by the time she could retrieve it, Uletka and the bird were gone.

The blackbird took Uletka on his back and flew to the branch of a tree. Leaves all around hid them, and from the high branch Uletka could see over the countryside. They were almost out of the forest.

"I can see the tower," she said. "We are close enough to reach it before the witch if we hurry."

They flew to the tower with the witch close behind. Uletka hurried inside, followed by the witch. She ran upstairs to the highest room. Through a high window she heard the blackbird calling her name.

"Quickly, Uletka! Climb on my back."

She did, and the bird flew out the window with her. He set her down outside the door of the tower.

"Slam it. Quick!"

As the tower door clanged shut on the witch, she disappeared forever in a puff of smoke, and the Princess regained her right size.

Uletka rejoined her mom and dad, who were overjoyed to see her. Her dear friend the blackbird nested in a high bush near the castle. The two were friends forever after.

Escape
to
Erehwon!

By George A. Smith

"Happy birthday!" Maria cried, bursting into her brother's bedroom.

"Oh, no!" Wayne growled. "You've messed up my program again!"

"Sorry! What is it—Space Invaders?" Maria asked.

"It's a program for four dimensions. I bet you don't even know what I mean!" said Wayne.

"I do!" Maria protested, and her fingers danced over the keyboard. "See? All you have to do is push ESCAPE . . ."

Bright lights dazzled Wayne's eyes as he landed on a thick, springy white mat. Beside him, Maria squealed in dismay.

"Where's our house?" Wayne shouted, leaping to his feet.

Thin, cold air smelled faintly of licorice. A fierce blue-white sun blazed above their heads. Distant mountains formed a long black wall against the horizon. Trees like partly unfolded blue umbrellas stretched toward the eggplant-colored sky.

Wayne pinched his arm. "It's not a dream!"

The ground heaved. A strange object, like a badly made doughnut, popped out and rolled toward them. They ran into a forest, leaving the round creature behind.

"This isn't Earth!" Wayne gasped, sounding both excited and scared.

"Where are we?"

"On another planet, Maria."

"Where's Earth, then?"

"Up there. It might be light-years away!" Wayne panted, leaning against a slim blue tree trunk. "How do we find our way back?" he wondered aloud.

"Maybe we should look for footprints."

"Good idea, Maria."

They looked in vain. The white squashy plants had swallowed their footprints.

"I'm thirsty," Maria said, pointing. "That dark line might be a stream."

It was. Crystal clear water bubbled along the bottom of a narrow gully. Lying down, Maria pushed aside orange creepers. "A snake!" she squealed.

"Where?"

"It's invisible!"

Wayne carefully moved orange leaves. He touched something cold . . . hard . . . T-shaped. He couldn't see it, but his fingers felt it. So did Maria's. "Know what it is, Maria?"

"I don't know. But I've touched one before."

"Of course you have. It's a garden faucet, and that snake is really a hose," Wayne said.

"I can feel it, but I can't see it."

"It's a piece of our world in this world," Wayne explained excitedly.

"Maybe there's more," Maria said.

Softly, delicately, carefully, they searched.

"Here's some wood, Wayne."

"A fence."

"It's like being blindfolded," Maria whispered.

"We can't see it, but our fingers tell us it's there."

"Which fence?" Maria asked.

They looked about slowly. There were no doughnut creatures in sight. "Keep searching," Wayne said.

As if catching invisible butterflies, they tickled the air. Soon Wayne said excitedly, "I've found a gate."

Maria joined him. "A big metal gate."

"There's a number . . . I think it's 38. Our house is number 28," Wayne said.

"I wish I could see it!"

"If we find our house, Maria, maybe I can reverse the computer program."

"Of course! It was the computer that brought us here," Maria gasped.

"We must get back!" Wayne said urgently. "Mom comes home at four o'clock. If she finds the computer left on . . ."

"She'll switch it off!"

"And we'll never ever get back home!" Wayne finished.

Maria's watch showed 3:37 P.M.

It was a race against time. With outstretched hands, they started a desperate search. Their fingertips brushed invisible wood, leaves, and a furriness that bounced away from Maria's hand. "A cat, I think," she whispered.

"A wall," Wayne said gruffly.

Together they felt along the invisible wall.

"A trellis, with roses . . . ouch!"

"Number 38's prize roses," Wayne said.

3:42 P.M.

Wayne's fingertips touched wood. "The fence between 38 and 36."

Maria whispered, "Which way?"

"That way, about five lots. Come on!"

As they walked over springy white plants, through unseen fences, Maria bent and picked up a curious object.

3:50 P.M.

Something light and silken as a breeze moved away from Wayne's fingertips. "Laundry on a clothesline! What do you think?"

Maria brushed the air lightly. "Babies' booties: Mrs. Barrow's new baby."

Mrs. Barrow lived at number 30.

The wild white sun slipped down toward the shadowy mountains.

3:54 P.M.

"Here's wire netting!" Maria exclaimed.

"Dad's aviary!"

"Which way now?"

"Across the driveway, through the living room, through Dad's study, to my bedroom, and we're there," Wayne said, feeling for invisible walls of brick and mortar.

Metal, warmth, smoothness.

"Mom's home! Here's her car in the drive!"

3:56 P.M.

"Quick, Maria."

They felt their way through their own home.

"Stop!" Wayne felt carefully under his feet.

Tiles. Bath. Soap holder. "Through here, Maria."

Maria, face pink and flushed, looked again at the weird white plants, blue trees, and purple sky.

"I wish we could stay," she said.

"We'll come back, with a camera," Wayne promised. "Here's my table. I can feel my disk box!"

He took two slow steps.

3:59 P.M.

His fingers tapped invisible keys.

4:00 P.M.

As they stood gasping in front of the computer, safely back home, Maria showed Wayne what she had picked up. It was a child's toy, a small animal carved from rubbery wood, with a long giraffe neck, two tails, and six legs.

"We weren't dreaming," Wayne whispered.

INSIDE OUTSIDE

OUTSIDE IN

By Janet S. Anderson

"Jen! Wake up! Please, wake up now!"

Jen opened one eye. The room was full of sunlight. It was also full of trees and grass and yellow dandelions. "Oh, no!" She shut her eye again. "I forgot, didn't I? I forgot the switch." She tried to pull the blanket up, but the blanket was gone. The bed was gone. Of course.

She felt a tug on her hand. "Please, Jen. Please get up." This time Jen opened both eyes. Jess was sitting next to her in a pile of leaves.

"At least it's a nice day this time," said Jen. "Last time I forgot the switch, it rained all day. The house was full of puddles." She sat up. "Is there anything to eat?"

Jess's hand unfolded its offering of crushed berries. "And there might be some carrots ready, out in the living room. But, Jen, what about Aunt Margaret? She won't laugh when she wakes up like Aunt May did last time. Aunt Margaret hates the outdoors and surprises like this."

"She hates everything," said Jen. "But we promised Mama we'd be polite to her. I just wish Mama was coming home today instead of tomorrow. Why does this always happen when Mama's off helping Grandma?"

"Because," said Jess, "when Mama's here, she remembers the switch. That's why."

Jen jumped up and ran to the window. The grass felt soft under her bare feet. "It's all out there," she said. "The beds and the table and the . . ."

"And the refrigerator," said Jess. "If we could only get out." She grabbed the window sash and tugged.

"You know we can't," said Jen. "We tried last time. You know very well that we're stuck until tomorrow morning."

"But Aunt Margaret's going to wake up any minute! Jen, I'm scared."

Jen tiptoed around the pile of rustling leaves and peered into the next room. "Well, she's sleeping hard enough now. Look, she's snoring so hard that the bush is shaking."

"Shhh," whispered Jess. She pulled Jen down the mossy hall toward the living room. "We've got to find the switch and get it switched back. We've just got to."

Jen shook her head. "We looked last time, remember? It should be on the wall in the kitchen, but everything on the walls is outside now. We can't reach it." She pulled a tiny carrot out of the garden and brushed off the dirt. "This garden's a mess. Look at all the weeds."

"Yes," said Jess. "And do you know what will happen if Aunt Margaret wakes up and sees them? She'll make us spend the whole day pulling weeds."

"Yes, and raking leaves out of our bedroom," said Jen. "And mopping up the creek in the kitchen. You're right. We've got to do something."

"But what?" said Jess. They sat for a few minutes, munching berries and thinking.

"What about magic?" said Jen. "Magic's good for a lot of things."

Jess immediately jumped up and waved her arms. "Astabasta-boo!" she said. Jess spun around three times and pointed at the garden. "Go back, granola!" she said.

A worm poked its head out of the soft dirt, looked at them, and poked it back in. A tear dripped down Jess's cheek.

"This is no time to cry," said Jen. "Time," she repeated. "Jess, what time is it?"

"Almost time for Aunt Margaret to wake up," wailed Jess. "She wakes up at exactly 8 o'clock every morning."

"Time. A clock," said Jen. "I need a clock. Where's a clock?"

"All the clocks are outside," said Jess, sniffing. "Except . . ."

"Except what?" said Jen.

"Except Aunt Margaret's watch," said Jess. "The one she always wears."

"Well," said Jen, "we've got to get it." She strode down the hall toward the guest room where Aunt Margaret was sleeping.

"What are you going to do?" said Jess. "Jen, don't go in there. Don't!"

"We've got to," said Jen. "We've got to turn the hands on Aunt Margaret's watch ahead. We've got to make it tomorrow in the house instead of today. Then the house will switch back by itself."

Jess was shaking her head. "Look!" she whispered. Aunt Margaret was no longer snoring. Her eyelids were beginning to flutter open. In one swift movement Jen was beside her, sliding the metal band of the watch off her wrist.

"Whaa . . . ?" said Aunt Margaret. But the watch's hands were already beginning to turn. 9, 10, 11, 12. Aunt Margaret struggled to sit up. Jen turned faster.

4, 5, 6, 7. The room began to darken. Far overhead a star sprang out. Aunt Margaret drowsed back into her pile of leaves. 12, 1, 2, 3. Jen and Jess yawned, and as they sank into the tall grass, the watch dropped out of Jen's hand.

Slowly the darkness lifted. The house was silent except for the quiet breathing of three sleeping figures. And then a door clicked open. A bar of sunlight slipped into the room, and with it . . .

"Jen, Jess." The voice was soft and warm. "Jen, wake up. It's Mama." She smiled as two pairs of arms lifted in sleepy hugs. "What in the world are you doing sleeping on the rug?"

"Mama, you're home. It's tomorrow, and you're home."

Mama picked up the watch from the floor next to the bed. Gently, she pulled a long piece of grass out of Jen's tangled hair. She sighed, but as Jen and Jess pulled her out of the guest room and into the bright kitchen, she was smiling.

They were all smiling.

Mama was home, and in and out were back where they belonged.

The Dragon, the Unicorn, and the Caterpillar

By Vivian Vande Velde

Once upon a time a certain wizard realized he had run out of magic. He had used too many spells that day.

Everything would be fine again in the morning, but meanwhile he had to find a nice dry place to spend the night.

He went to a nearby cave opening and called, "Halloo! Anybody home?"

"If you please, sir," a tiny voice whispered, "there's only me—a furry little caterpillar."

The wizard didn't especially like caterpillars, but he said, "It's getting dark and beginning to drizzle. May I spend the night in your cave?"

"Oh, certainly," said the caterpillar. The wizard sat in the corner farthest away from him.

"If you please, sir," the caterpillar called after a while, "if you're hungry, I could share my dinner— a nice fresh mulberry leaf and a crispy twig."

"No thanks," said the wizard. "I'll just quietly go to sleep now."

"Yes, sir. Thank you very much, sir," the caterpillar said, but the wizard was already asleep.

Soon he was awakened by a loud roar and a burst of flame.

"Hey!" yelled the wizard.

"Eeek!" cried the caterpillar.

"Oh," said a large dragon who had entered the cave, "I didn't realize anybody was here." He settled down with his chin on his paws, and the wizard had to move over to avoid the dragon's tail. "I just needed to get in from the rain, and this looked like a comfortable, warm place."

"Sir? Excuse me, sir?" the caterpillar called. "Would you like to share my dinner?"

The dragon wasn't really hungry, but he asked, "Do you have a nice thick steak back there?"

"No, but I have a mulberry leaf and a twig."

"Don't bother me with leaves and twigs," the dragon snapped.

"No, sir. Pardon me, sir," the caterpillar said.

The wizard drifted back to sleep until someone at the cave entrance yelled in, "Yoo-hoo! Does anyone live here?"

"Yes," the furry little caterpillar answered. "If you please, sir, I do."

A unicorn entered the cave, then stopped, startled by the dragon. "Oh," he said, "you have such a surprisingly tiny voice."

"Don't be ridiculous," the dragon replied. "That was just the furry little caterpillar who lives here. There's some man here, too."

"I'm hungry. Do they have anything to eat?" asked the unicorn.

"Excuse me. It's just me again," said the caterpillar. "Yes, I have a bit of leaf and a twig left, sir."

"No thanks. I eat only nectar and water lilies," said the unicorn.

The wizard was about to fall asleep again when the unicorn said, "Such a nasty night! I was afraid of getting caught in the rain and soiling my beautiful white coat."

"It's very pretty," the caterpillar agreed politely.

"Humph!" said the dragon. "Scales are better."

"Scales?" the unicorn repeated. *"Scales?"*

"Certainly. You should see my scales shine in the sun. They sparkle."

The wizard's eyes grew heavy, and his head started to nod.

"A horn!" the unicorn cried, waking everyone up with a start. "You don't have a horn like this! Look how pretty. You, caterpillar, isn't this a lovely horn?"

"Yes, sir. Very nice, sir."

"Oh, what does a caterpillar know?" the dragon said. "If you want to talk about perfect shape—take a look at these fine wings." He lifted them and almost bumped into the wizard, who crawled closer to the caterpillar to get out of the way.

The dragon made a sound like a cat's purr. "Oh, but I forgot, unicorn. You don't have any wings."

The unicorn sniffed and turned his back.

The wizard dozed off until the unicorn said, "Everyone loves unicorns. People try to catch us all the time because we're so pretty."

"Big deal," the dragon answered. "People run away from dragons because we're so fierce." He growled, sending a tongue of flame into the dawn.

"Aargh!" the wizard screamed. "Would you two please be quiet? You vain, noisy, inconsiderate . . ." He had to stop because he couldn't think of an insult good enough for them.

The unicorn lowered his head, ready to charge, and the dragon, his eyes glowing angrily, struggled to his feet.

But at the same time, the sun finally peeked over the edge of the world, and the wizard felt his magic power return.

He pointed at the dragon and said a secret word.

The dragon shrank and shrank and shrank until he was nothing more than the creature that has come to be called a dragonfly. His sparkling wings flapped hurriedly, taking him away from the cave.

The wizard pointed at the unicorn and said another secret word.

The unicorn started to spread out. His sleek body became lumpy, and his golden horn a short, fat thing on the nose of the world's first rhinoceros. With an embarrassed grunt, he left the cave as quickly as his stumpy legs would take him.

The wizard turned to the quaking caterpillar and pointed a finger.

"Eeek! I didn't do anything!" the caterpillar cried, covering his eyes with his front feet. But by then the wizard had already said a third secret word.

The caterpillar blinked, because somehow, unexplainably, the world was blue. He lowered his legs and saw that they had changed to beautiful bright blue wings.

"What am I?" he cried, joyfully leaping into the air and fluttering into the warm sunlight.

"A butterfly," the wizard's voice answered. But it was only his voice that remained, for by then the wizard had gone.

Uncle Er's Magic

By Juanita Barrett Friedrichs

Rosemary's great-uncle Erwin was a magician. Not just the rope-and-card trick, rabbit-out-of-a-hat kind. His talents went far beyond that. You don't find many magicians around today who can begin to compare with Rosemary's great-uncle Er.

Rosemary always went to Uncle Er when she had a problem. So when Rosemary and her younger sister, Laura, got into a fight and Laura threw her sneakers at Rosemary and Rosemary said she was never going to speak to Laura again, much less share a room with her, Rosemary ran straight to Uncle Er.

"You can do anything, Uncle Er," she began. "I know you can. You are the best magician in the whole wide world."

"Never mind flattery," growled Uncle Er. "Just get to the point."

"I want you to turn me into a zebra so Mom won't make me share a room with Laura anymore. If I were a zebra, I could sleep in the garage."

Uncle Er raised his eyebrows and turned down the corners of his mustache. His expression was not at all encouraging.

"If you'd rather change me into an elephant or a giant panda, that would be OK, too."

"Zebra, elephant, panda . . . ," muttered Uncle Er. "It's all too easy. If you want that kind of magic, go to one of those rope-and-card trick, rabbit-out-of-a-hat magicians. They're listed in the Yellow Pages."

Rosemary really hoped she hadn't insulted her great-uncle.

"Well, Uncle Er, what do *you* suggest?"

Uncle Er closed his eyes.

Rosemary waited.

"Got it!" Uncle Er's eyes popped open. He snapped his fingers. "Bring me a pair of Laura's shoes—the ones she threw at you."

When Uncle Er gives an order, you'd better follow it, no matter how wild it sounds. So Rosemary rushed up to the bedroom, grabbed Laura's sneakers, and hurried back to her uncle. She was glad no one had seen her.

"Now put them on."

"But they're too small."

"Never mind. Put them on anyway."

It was a squeeze, but Rosemary finally managed it. She stood bent-toed and teetering in front of Uncle Er. "Now," said Uncle Er, "I am going to turn you into Laura."

"Into LAURA! I don't want to be Laura! Please, Uncle Er, boa constrictor, warthog, three-toed sloth, Gila monster— anything but Laura."

"Laura!" said Uncle Er. "And no arguments."

Great-Uncle Er, magician, gave Rosemary a look that sent vibrations right through to her bones.

"You are a small, young girl, age seven and a half to be exact."

Rosemary, who under normal circumstances was ten and tall for her age, felt herself shrinking. Soon she felt small, like Laura. Now she could wiggle her toes inside Laura's sneakers.

"You are in second grade, and there are a lot of things you don't know yet," continued Uncle Er.

Suddenly Rosemary's head felt like a pail with holes in the bottom. The entire multiplication table, fractions, long division, the geography of North America, and several hundred spelling words from *absurd* to *zany* leaked out.

"Rosemary won't let you help with the rowboat because you tried hammering a nail and hit your thumb," said Uncle Er. "She says you're all thumbs."

Rosemary didn't dare look at her hands. They felt lumpy and uncomfortable, as if she had ten thumbs and had whammed each one with a hammer.

"Rosemary doesn't want to share a room with you because she says you're not grown-up enough. She tells everybody what a dummy you are."

Rosemary couldn't stand it any longer. "She's mean, Uncle Er! Rosemary's not fair. I'll fix *her!*"

Rosemary reached down and yanked off one of her sneakers without bothering to untie it. She waved it in the air. "Where's Rosemary?" she yelled.

"Take off your other sneaker and you'll find her," said Uncle Er calmly.

Rosemary pulled off the other sneaker. "Hey! What's happening?"

She stared down at her bare feet. They had grown from size one to size four in the blink of an eye, and the rest of her was struggling to catch up. Her head buzzed like a vacuum cleaner, sucking up multiplication tables, fractions, and so on.

Rosemary dropped the sneakers on the floor. "I *am* Rosemary!" she said in amazement. Then she felt a stab of pain in one thumb as if she had hit it with a hammer. "Or am I Laura?"

"If you ask me," said Uncle Er, "from now on you are a little bit of both."

"Huh?" muttered Rosemary.

Uncle Er frowned. "You have just witnessed the most difficult, challenging, spectacular piece of magic imaginable, and all you have to say is 'Huh?' Put on your shoes."

Rosemary bent over to tie her shoelaces. When she straightened up, Uncle Er had gone.

Now that she was wearing her own shoes, Rosemary felt more like herself. She headed for the bedroom to return Laura's sneakers.

Laura met her on the stairs. "There they are. You stole my sneakers!"

"I just borrowed them for a minute."

"What for?" Laura looked at her suspiciously.

"For a little of Uncle Er's magic."

"Uncle Er never does his special magic for *me*," said Laura.

"I bet he would if you asked him." Rosemary winked at her little sister. "You can even borrow my new sneakers."

After that Rosemary forgot all about wanting to be a zebra. But she never quite forgot what it had been like to be Laura. Every once in a while, especially on cranky days, Rosemary got a slight thumbache, just to remind her. Her Laura Thumb, Uncle Er called it.

SPACE DAY

By Eve Bunting

I hated not having any friends. Mom said it would be all right when school started. Terrific! But this was summer. School wouldn't start for another six weeks.

I headed along Beach Street toward the pier. I was carrying my fishing pole the way a warrior carries a spear.

Something was going on in the Beach Street Library. Kids were streaming in the doors. They were all dressed up, like Halloween. A robot skipped up the path. A guy in a red shirt had a Wolfman head. I saw the banner over the door.

SPACE DAY
COSTUMES • PRIZES
COME ONE, COME ALL

"Hey," I thought, "it says come one, come all. I'm one. No problem." I pushed open the door.

Inside it was like *Star Wars*. Honest.

"Would you like some Galaxy Punch?" a lady asked. She wore high heels and a box on her head. I figured she was the librarian.

"Yes, please, ma'am," I said politely.

Cardboard stars were hung all around the room. A girl with Dracula teeth slurped at Galaxy Punch.

"You're supposed to be dressed up," she said.

I took a handful of Cosmic Cookies. "I'm a star fisherman," I said.

I looked around. In here I was so ordinary I was weird. Then I saw another ordinary guy. He was wearing blue jeans and his own head. I edged over to his corner.

"Want a Cosmic Cookie?" I asked him. I didn't blame him for shaking his head. They were pretty nasty-looking from being squished in my hand.

He looked at my rod. "You going fishing?"

"Yes," I said.

"Where do you go?"

"Just on the pier," I said. "I'm new here, so I don't know the good spots."

"Yeah?" The guy said with a grin. "I'm just here for the day myself."

The librarian clapped her hands. "It's time to judge the costumes."

"Who do you think's going to win?" I asked.

"They're all terrible," he said. "Insulting."

We stood watching as the robot took first prize.

"It should have been the dark-haired girl with the crown," I said.

"It should have been you."

I laughed. "Sure."

He wasn't laughing. "Why do humans always make us look so freaky?"

"Us? Humans?"

"You humans call us 'little green men' and 'creatures from outer space.' Do I look like a creature?"

I stared at him. Was he kidding?

He glanced at the clock. "I have to go. Our space boat leaves in ten minutes. I'll get in some fishing on the way home."

I tried to laugh. "You mean spaceship, don't you?"

"Spaceship is a human word. It's not ours." He sounded mad.

"Sorry," I mumbled. Was this guy for real?

"You want me to come fishing with you tomorrow?" he asked.

I nodded.

"I'll come back down then. See you on the pier at three o'clock."

The librarian was standing in front of us. "More punch and cookies?"

"No thanks," I said. I turned around. "Would you like some?" I asked.

There was nobody there. He must have slipped away. Or disappeared. Or melted. Naw! That was crazy. Anyway, I'd see him tomorrow. I wouldn't mind having a space boy for a friend. I wouldn't mind having a friend. Period. Especially one like this. A good kidder. With a neat sense of humor.

I wanted to rush outside right away. But I knew I should be polite, so I told the librarian my name and where I lived and stuff like that.

When I got out, there was no sign of the guy. I looked up at the sky. Actually, I felt goofy for even looking. Of course there was no space boat. There was just a dopey-shaped cloud floating by. With a fishing pole sticking out of the end of it.